First published in 2015 by © Rockpool Children's Books Ltd.

This edition published in 2015 by Rockpool Children's Books Ltd. in
association with Albury Books.
Albury Court, Albury, Thame
OX9 2LP, United Kingdom

www.AlburyBooks.com

For orders: Kuperard Publishers and Distributors
+44 (0) 208 4462440

A CIP catalogue record of this book is available
from the British Library.

Printed and bound in China

ISBN 978-1-906081-90-4 (Paperback)

rockpool
children's books

Albury Books

Stuart Trotter

Polar White

It was snowing outside.

"A perfect day for the seaside,"
said Polar White to Rusky.
He packed his beach bag.
He had a bucket, a spade,
some sandwiches and a drink.

Rusky had his ball.

Polar White and little Ted got on
the sledge, and Rusky pulled them
whooshhh...
across the snow!

They
swishhhhed...
through an ice cave.

They
whooshhhed...
down a snowy slope.

At the seaside, Polar White made a
snow castle. It wasn't very good.

Rusky tried to make a snow husky,
by rolling a large snowball!

Polar White took his boat
down to the seashore.
He knelt down and gazed
at his reflection
in the water.
Suddenly...

..."Boo!"

said Walter Walrus.
"Coming for a swim?"

Polar White hung on tight, as
Walter swam deep into the ocean,

through shoals of shiny, silvery fish...

...and alongside Harry the humpback whale!

They leapt over a small iceberg...

...and swam under a huge one!

While Polar White and Ted got dry,
Walter took Rusky for a ride.
Rusky didn't like getting wet,
so he sat on Walter's head.
"Woo hoo!"
he whooped.

Their swim had made them all
very hungry, so they tucked into
Polar White's picnic.

"Yummy,"
munched Walter.

"Yummy," pecked seagull.

They waved goodbye to Walter
and got back on the sledge.
The swishing and swooshing
of the sledge across the snow
made Polar White fall fast asleep.

What a lovely day
at the seaside!

"Huh, it might have been a
good day for some!"
muttered a very soggy Ted.